WHOM THE KISKADEES CALL

CHURAUMANIE BISSUNDYAL

PEEPAL TREE

First published in Great Britain in 1994
Peepal Tree Books
17 King's Avenue
Leeds LS6 1QS
England

ISBN 0 948833 72 6

1.

Challu walked up the steps of Belmonte Hotel, his head hanging, his eyes sharp for anything new. The woman mopping the stairs lifted her eyes at his approach, straightened her back and stood as if frozen. Then she wrung the mop in the bucket and dabbed ineffectually at the floor as she appraised him from head to toe, squeezing herself in against the wall as he passed. He did not look at her. He did not have to look at her to see her. Habit had tutored him like a keen dog to sense every woman there, whether she had been there a full year or had arrived only the day before.

When he reached the top of the stairs, the woman behind the bar counter saw him. The laughter on her face erased to leave a blank, unruffled sheet. The thin woman leaning on the counter fell silent too. He stood before the bar and the woman behind it fished out a bottle of high wine from under the counter and pushed it in front of him. He paid, picked it up and moved to a solitary table in the corner and sat there, chin cupped in palms on propped elbows. It was the corner next to the toilets, whose smell alone ensured that no one else would sit there.

The thin woman broke her frozen posture and moved to serve him. She brought a glass, a large bottle of water and smashed ice in a rust-stained plastic bowl. For a moment she stood over him in motionless absorption. He sensed her blank face staring at him uncertainly. He removed the hand propping his chin, but did not lift his eyes from the table. When the woman left he poured and drank.

The strained atmosphere did not last long. The concentrate of Challu's presence soon became diluted in the arrival of other men. The clamour of the women filled the hallway again. Challu twisted his lips and tried not to listen, but the sounds still came to him. He drank more, hoping that he would not hear, but the voices still came, blasting him with images of every conceivable act performed by the women in this hotel.

'Alyou ain't going to bathe?' a gruff voice rasped.

Challu's lips twisted in greater revulsion.

The voice came again, deeper, gathering more force.

'Alyou ain't going to wash alyou skin?'

Now the sounds of the women petered out and yielded to the noises of the traffic outside. Two of the women, who were sweeping the hall, dropped their brooms and turned in the direction of the voice.

'Why alyou stare at me like statue? I is no jumbie. I just want to know if alyou going to wash alyou skin.'

One of the women sucked her teeth. Challu knew it was Sugar Plum, plump and dowdy from North West District.

'Boss Man, you can't curse we so.' This was Nice Gyal, from Non Pariel. She had a sharp tongue. Once she had broken the head of a bullying policeman with a rum bottle. 'So alyou ain't know alyou duty,' Boss Man said more softly. 'It ten o'clock already. Customer start come in.'

'Why you ain't wash you own skin?' Sugar Plum raged.

Boss Man swelled up in anger again. 'Because I don't do business with me skin. It alyou who have to clean up alyou skin to win lottery today. Today is St. Valentine.'

'It you who should go and bathe for St. Valentine,' Nice Gyal protested.

Boss Man exploded like a raked ants' nest. 'Don't take alyou eye and pass me. I is the boss for Belmonte Hotel.'

'Me eye and you eye never been for a race,' Sugar Plum teased. 'You wash you skin first; then we going to wash we skin after.'

The other women tittered. Boss Man grabbed a chair and hurled it at Sugar Plum, who dodged and screamed. Nice Gyal, as ever, interceded.

'Why you pelt the chair on she for?'

'What right she have to give me mouth for?'

'How you know I going to win lottery for St Valentine?' Sugar Plum retorted, cowering behind Nice Gyal.

'Because you get luck to win things on day like this.'

Sugar Plum pinched at Nice Gyal's arm for support. 'You hear how he twisting the story? If I tell you about he and Tiger Cat...'

Boss man reared up like a labaria. 'Done this story!'

'Done what story?' Sugar Plum jeered.

'Done this story. Done this story and go and bathe alyou skin and don't cock alyou tail here as if you is the boss for this damn hotel.'

'Who you talking to?' Nice Gyal challenged. 'You think we make out of iron? We been working up to four o'clock last night, you know. Short-time work is no sport.'

Boss Man opened his eyes wide; the tension in his skin made the scar on his face look even more grotesque than usual.

'What you talkin' there is rass!' he spat. 'As far as I is concern alyou is a set of dirty people sleeping whole night with all kind of men and don't want to bathe.'

Nice Gyal was surprised to feel real anger shoot through her, but she masked her feelings with a smile.

'You *dress* up nice, Boss Man,' she said, 'but you bathe you skin this morning?'

Boss Man felt the blow. His shirt-jac, unchanged for two weeks, was dirty and smelly. 'That is me business. I is Boss Man. And is only Boss Man give orders.'

Sugar Plum relished trapping Boss Man in a helpless rage and then seeing him slump in its aftermath. She would add fuel to the fire, the verse she had for him, told only in private to the other women. She had been waiting for the right time to strike.

'Boss Man, I want to tell you something,' she started, her head in a mischievous incline.

'What?'

'Go and wash you skin, Boss Man,' she sang out.

> 'Wash it with full speed
> like a donkey-cart
> with no wheel.
> Wash it with dettol
> and iodine
> and foam
> to make mad-men
> run and scream...'

This made the women rock and wheeze with laughter and when they would not stop, Boss Man let go another string of obscenities. This made the women laugh more.

'Get alyou tail out of here!' he yelled, foot-stomping, 'or else I break alyou stinking behinds!'

The women ignored him and joined Sugar Plum in the tempo of the verse. This provoked Boss Man to even greater threats of violence. But the women sang merrily with clapping hands and filed up the stairs leading to the upper rooms.

It was in these upper rooms where business was done. Challu raised his eyes from the table and surveyed the women. Pity mixed with loathing. Beneath the women's screen of gaiety he saw the scourge of overwork, venereal diseases, beatings and humiliations. He spat, watching until the skirt of the last woman swished and disappeared through the door.

The woman behind the bar was trying to stifle an out-
burst of laughter, her hands covering her mouth. Boss
Man was staring at her.

'Alyou see how these girls take them eye and pass me,
Reenee?'

Reenee couldn't restrain her laughter any longer.

'You cause it on you own self because you show them
no respect.'

'What right they have to make calypso out of me for?'

'The girls just making joke with you, man.'

'And what about that nonsense with Tiger Cat?'

Reenee cackled. 'The girls just want to hurt you head,
man. Don't bother with them.'

Boss Man pushed his hands in his trouser pockets and
began pacing in awkward frenzy.

'That is defamation of character. I going to consult me
lawyer. Big lawyer I have. Better know that.'

'If you do that,' Reenee said, 'people going to think the
story true.'

Boss Man stormed again. 'I is a man. What they take
me for... a fucking 'maphrodite?'

'If you is a man, you don't have to open you mouth so
big to tell the whole world.'

'If I is not a man, then you won't have been me woman.
You know you is me love in bed,' he added with pleading
affection.

'Who *is* you love in bed?' Reenee raged. 'You have you
wife.'

He came closer to her. 'Wife?' he said in pained reflection. 'If I have a wife, she playing the fool.'

Before Reenee could reply, a tall, muscular man, shirt-less, came in, a matchstick stuck between his teeth, cigarettes perched behind each ear.

'Boss,' he growled, 'how much you think we should charge for the door-fee?'

Boss Man started to think. 'You should charge some-thing big,' he said gravely. Then he let his hand fall affably on his chucker-out's back. 'What happen with you, Tiger Cat? You ain't know today is St. Valentine?'

Tiger Cat chewed at his matchstick. 'How much so?'

Boss Man's face contorted with thought. 'You can put it ten dollar a head.'

Tiger Cat stopped chewing. 'Awright. I think that price is not too hot.' He took a cigarette from behind his ear and lit it. 'But I ain't seeing the girls around.'

'You know they always have lots of style,' Boss Man said bitterly.

Tiger Cat took a heavy draw on his cigarette and laughed out the smoke from his mouth. 'They going to make some big draw tonight.'

Boss Man frowned. 'Big draw, eh?. These girls take them eye and pass me. They say I is a hermaphrodite.'

Tiger Cat crushed the cigarette under his foot and con-vulsed with laughter. 'Don't take them girls serious, boss. They making joke with you.'

Boss Man opened his eyes wide. 'Joke? I ain't mincing joke with business.'

'That is small potato.' Tiger Cat made a dismissive

gesture and strode, heavy-legged, across to the door where the men queued up for admission and posted himself on a drinks-crate at the entrance.

Boss Man turned to Reenee and looked earnestly at her for support. 'You see, he too playing the ass with heself.'

Reenee smiled but said nothing. Boss Man clucked his tongue at her and strode across to the exit where his car was parked. The engine revved and he was gone.

The women trickled back in rapid springing steps through the door, in a blaze of vermillion and white dresses, their cheeks rouged rose-pink, lips glazed in red, pink and sometimes black, hair arranged in a diversity of styles and perfume reeking from their bosoms in a clamour of brands. No trace of fatigue; they were beautiful damsels of the moonlight now, fresh virgins for free spenders to conquer.

The stereo set was switched on and music blared. The men were coming in hordes now with loud and rapid voices and hot glances at the women. There were men with meagre paypackets from the sugar estates, trawler men smelling of fish, men from the nearby lumber-yards with big deals in stolen timber; rice barons with arrogant cheques: some boastful, some quiet, but all with one thing in mind.

Boss Man came back an hour or so later looking fresh and well-attired in a lily-white shirt-jac suit and a bright smile embossed on his face. Challu heard his voice when the music paused for a moment. He spat again in revulsion. Boss Man knew how to put on a false face to impress, knew how to exaggerate the corporation of his body with a tight shirt over the distended balloon of his belly to indicate money. He would even oil the bald patch on his head to a shiny glaze.

'Big belly and bald head mean a lot of money,' he would say. 'It make you look like a billionaire.'

Challu heard Tiger Cat's bawdy laughter; he was glowing with excitement over the rapid flow of money at the door. When the men complained of the high charges he would say: 'Today is a big day, man. St. Valentine's Day. You ain't know?'

Sugar Plum heard him and winked. Good business tonight. A lot of customers were already there, a lot more coming in. She would get a big slice of the cake tonight. When the men were drunk she would run through their pockets and make her haul. She winked again. Tiger Cat winked back. Good business!

The tables were now full, bunches of men perching everywhere, the women squeezed in close between them, a rivalry of voices bargaining for the best deal. A chair was pushed aside; more followed. A man and a woman disappeared to the rooms upstairs; more men and women followed. Before too long the men came trickling back looking spent; when the women reappeared, they were restored, it seemed, to virginal freshness.

Challu poured and drank. Customers edged past him to relieve themselves in the toilets, and then hurried away to escape the stink and Challu's unwavering look of disdain.

The afternoon wore to evening and evening to night.
The lights came on and the hall swirled with kaleidoscopic
colours. The women spread their splendid wings and
exploded with butterfly charm and the men responded
with aggressive talk and displays of power. Rivalries
began. Men possessed their women tightly, yet others
took them to bed. Jealousies sparked. A fight began.
Blows were struck and knives were drawn. The music
stopped. Screams and curses came from the women. The
fight was broken up; the music switched back on. Challu
watched, poured and drank. This tedious drama was
replayed each night.

Dawn approached unnoticed. An air of languor over-
came the hall. The men were drunk and the women had
extracted enough takings for the night. Tiger Cat smiled
knowingly and the stereo set was switched off. At this
sign of imminent ejection, some men became boisterous
and started cursing.

'We closing up now,' Tiger Cat told them. 'Business
done.'

The men cursed louder and one short, fat man lost
command over himself, broke a bottle on the floor and
hurled the fanged remnants at Tiger Cat. It missed him
and crashed against the wall. Tiger Cat's smile froze and
he stalked over and grabbed the man by the throat and
began pumelling him with his fist. The man screamed out
in pain at every blow and, when he could bear it no more,
bawled out that he was sorry. Other men pleaded for him
and Tiger Cat stayed his arm and glared at him with flar-

ing nostrils. Then he pushed the fat man away to fall, flail-
ing, on the ground.

'You don't drink three-cents rum,' he scolded, ' and
play four-cents drunk in this place.'

If any of the others harboured the urge to fight they
gave no sign of it and the men milled out to the road in
sheepish good order.

Challu was the last to leave. He walked out, head-bent,
onto the street where the dogs barked and yelped. A horde
of prowling men approached but passed him without
incident, immersed in their own loud pursuits and blind
to his careless stagger. He knew their capacity for harm,
but he did not care, much less was afraid. In the silence of
the night there was a truce for survival.

In the starlit gloom of the new moon, a few blocks
ahead, Donkey Bugle Settlement loomed into view. At
first sight: a tight stitch of buildings shaping a huge sheet
of sea; later, as Challu crossed the High Bridge: a blur of
tattered shacks with flambeaux burning in the windows.

Noises from the houses ripped the silence: the cry of a
child; the harsh rebuke of a mother; a string of obscenities
from a husband; the terrified screams of a beaten wife.
Then the sounds would die and silence would return like
a balm on a weeping sore.

In the rum shop, men, throats overspent with liquor,
sang discordantly and drummed their hands on wooden
tables, their feet pounding the floor in frantic merriment.

As Challu turned from the public road into the alleyway where he lived, he stooped to roll up the legs of his trousers. The place was knee-deep in water. It had been raining incessantly over the past three months and there was no proper drainage. Mosquitoes thrived and malaria raged. Other diseases spread from the putrified and bloated carcasses floating in the water.

Challu had been living here for a full year now, in one of the rooms in the lower flat of a large overcrowded and dilapidated tenement. He rapped at the door where he lived. A voice mumbled something inside. He rapped again.

'Who that?'

'Me.'

A man opened the door and Challu entered.

'Put on the light,' Challu told him.

The man fumbled on the shelf and the sound of matches came. Then he lit a flambeaux on the floor and the room flared to an amber glow. He was shrouded to his neck in a jute bag and smelled heavily of liquor.

'What you cook?' Challu asked.

'Pumpkin and rice.' The other strangled a yawn and rubbed the sleep from his eyes.

'You been cooking pumpkin a whole month now.'

'Pumpkin good food.'

Challu ate the pumpkin and rice quietly and watched the column of red ants marching up and down the wall. The floods had brought them. Sometimes a centipede would come up too. Rats and cockroaches were persistent trespassers. They lived there untroubled, feeding on the scraps of food dumped in the biscuit tin near the kerosene stove.

The man could not bear the sting of Challu's silence. He lit a cigarette and drew heavily on it.

'You know I don't like it, Boras,' Challu said. 'I can't stand it.'

Boras crushed the cigarette and flicked it through the window.

'Awright,' he said, irked, 'Me going stop smoke here.'

When Challu had finished eating, they both lay down to sleep on the floor on jute bags, using flour-sacks stuffed with fowl-feathers as pillows.

'Me tearing skin these days,' Boras said.

'That good.'

'Me boss getting to like me head and he promote me to sell lumber.'

Challu gave a weak groan and turned on his stomach.

'Me making big money.'

'Oh,' Challu said curtly, stretched out his limbs and yawned.

'A chap called Shacks learning me how to cook up the books.'

'You awright then, man.' Challu yawned again.

'Me find a woman too.'

'You lucky,' Challu told him, wriggling his feet in the jute-bag and burying his head in his pillow.

'She name Florrie.'

'Nice name,' Challu said petulantly, hoping that Boras would stop.

'She remind me of me wife,' he persisted.

Challu sucked his teeth. 'Let me sleep, man.'

'She left me and gone with all me children. Good-good husband like me.'

Challu turned his face away from Boras and tried to blank his mind. He plunged deeper into his inner silence. They were all there again: Boss Man, Sugar Plum, Nice Gyal and Reenee. He slept away.

2

The following morning began well at Belmonte Hotel.
The women woke early, bathed and dressed. Their minds
were not on work; they would go downtown to shop
with last night's takings.

Nice Gyal emerged wearing a polka-dot mini-skirt and
a low-cut blouse.

'Things been bright last night,' she said to Reenee.

'Like you pick up something good?'

'Something good?' she skinned her eyes. 'Is seven
trawler men I knock down.'

'Gracious.'

'Gracious,' Nice Gyal repeated. 'I had to piss in their
vodka to make them lose their sense.'

'I hook up five Buck-man from the gold bush,' Sugar
Plum joined in.

'You had to piss in their vodka too?' Reenee asked.

'No, I gave them Guinness with condensed milk and a
raw egg in between.'

The women roared with more laughter.

Boss Man came in a few seconds later. He was wearing
one of his favourites — a blue shirt-jac suit with gold-

coated buttons. The fringe of hair around his bald patch was plastered with brilliantine and all the fingers on his left hand were beringed.

Sugar Plum sucked her teeth and left, but Boss Man was in too good spirits to respond to such trivialities. Instead he winked at Reenee.

'Like you is in a good mood this morning,' Reenee told him.

'I does always be in a good mood when I see you.'

'You is foolish.'

He took out his handkerchief and wiped the sweat off his face. 'You always like to play hard to get.'

'Who you want to get? I is nobody for you.'

'You is me love in bed.'

'You screw up my whole life and you call that love!'

Boss Man tightened his lips. 'Why you always remember the past?'

'You want me to forget what you done to me?'

'What I done to you? I bring you here and make you somebody.'

'You bring me to a stinking whore-house!'

'You is a cashier. You is not a whore.'

'I is a whore! You bring me here and not only rape me. You rape my whole life.'

'It was for you own good. I had to break you in for you to learn the job.'

She glared at him. 'Go away from here!'

'I is the boss. You can't talk to me like that.'

'You is a stinking ass.'

'I going to knock you off and find another girl.'

'I don't care. Do as you like.'

They quarrelled like this all day, until night fell and business resumed.

Challu came late that night. He did not go to the bar but direct to his corner. Reenee wondered why he behaved so oddly; she would challenge his cold, aloof air. She came out of the bar and brought him his high wine.

'This is on me,' she told him.

'No,' he shook his head, without looking up. 'I like to pay for what I drink.'

'You is a headstrong man.'

'I pay for what I drink.'

'I like to buy you a drink.'

He looked up at her. She was an attractive woman, he thought, full-breasted and supple.

'Why do you want to buy me a drink?'

'Because it going to make me feel nice.'

'Do you do this often with men?'

'No.' She sat down.

'Then why me?

'Because I want to know why you sit here.'

He poured and drank, forehead furrowed with thought.

'You drink?' he asked her.

'Yes. But not high wine.'

'What you drink?'

'Vodka with tomato juice.'

'So, I will buy you a drink.'

'Don't worry. I going to pour myself a shot and come back.'

She came back with the drink.

'You didn't tell me why you sit here.'

'The place stinks and nobody comes here.'

She looked at him, lips parted in surprise.

'I think you is funny. You dress like a working man but you talk like a lawyer man.'

He smiled.

'You like to be alone, eh?' she asked.

He nodded.

'I can see that for truth. You been coming here for a whole year now and you always sit alone.'

'I like it that way. I enjoy my high wine better.'

'I think something is wrong with you head.'

'Why do you say so?' he said, unruffled.

'Men come here only to take women to bed.'

'I come here to please myself in a different way.'

'You is a stupid man.'

'I see every side of the world here.'

'You should go preach in a church. Place like this not good for you.'

'I can't leave here. The pain of my past demands it.'

She laughed coarsely. 'Like you wife giving you worries or what, man?'

'My wife is dead.'

'Is that why you drinking so much high wine?'

'No.'

'Why?'

'Because I like it.'

This man was different and she wanted to know him. Each night after that she made a point of serving him herself and sitting down to speak with him. Each time they spoke, each time he dropped his guard a little, she liked him more. A week or so later they were friends.

One evening she rushed up to him as soon as he came in.

'Sugar Plum going to North West. She taking me with she. You want to go?'

He raised his head and looked at her with narrowed eyes. She thought for a moment he would say no. But his eyes relaxed again and he nodded in a slow, pleasant motion of assent.

They left the following Monday from Kingston Wharves, joining a boisterous crowd of passengers and porters struggling across a gang plank to the stern with their luggage.

The steamer was already choked with passengers, its floor littered with fruit skins, beer bottles and scraps of vegetables. Men talked at the top of their voices, swigged their drinks and urinated wherever they pleased. There were no deck chairs to sit on and the few available cabins had been booked long in advance. The toilets were dirty and smelly. Some of the passengers relieved themselves in paper-bags and threw them overboard.

At one-thirty, the steamer bellowed a signal for departure and, minutes later, it moored off the wharf in a tumult of good-byes from lookers-on and passengers.

At the point in the crossing where the Demerara River met the Atlantic Ocean, the steamer pitched and crashed into the waves. Challu hung his head over the rails and vomited.

'Like you get seasick, eh?' Reenee asked.

He vomited again.

'Take a good shot vodka,' Reenee offered. 'It going to help you.'

He drank the vodka but vomited in even sharper spasms.

'Take he downstairs,' Sugar Plum suggested.

Downstairs was worse. Though there were hammocks strung from the roof to lie in, below them were squealing pigs tied up on the floor. The place stank. Challu vomited more.

Reenee took him back to the deck and pulled together a few drinks-crates as a makeshift bed for him. She pillowed his head in her lap.

'I want a drink,' Challu moaned.

'What kind of drink you want?'

'High wine.'

She brought a bottle and Challu tilted it to his mouth and drank, then another and another. He drank a full half-bottle until he felt his mind floating softly in a sweet dizzy whirl. Everything was now receding and sleep came soon with the tender comfort of Reenee's thighs against his head. When he woke it was morning. The steamer was moving smoothly and Reenee was curled up into him.

She looked into his face and smiled. 'We in Waini River.'

He sat up and looked outside. The river was smooth and dark except where the sun stroked it with shafts of light. On the eastern shore, against the backdrop of mangrove trees, jostling crowds of sea-birds were pecking in the mud. Challu was absorbed by the beauty of this bird-freckled canvas.

A gunshot echoed somewhere in the trees and sent the birds in sudden flight.

'Really sweet out there, eh?' Reenee observed.

'I like it,' Challu said curtly, watching the birds flying.

'What make you like it?'

'Because man is not there.'

She did not understand.

'Somebody there shoot the birds,' she said.

'You're right. But here *belongs* to the birds.'

'Man is bad.'

'No, he is troubled. He feels violence is the only way to survive.'

They crossed the Mora Passage and entered the Barima River. Half-an-hour later, they were at Morawhanna Stelling.

Tuesday was business day at Morawhanna. An old man came and tried to sell a quake of crabs to Challu. 'One quake bundarie,' he pleaded. 'Only twenty dollar.'

Challu did not buy the crabs, but he gave the man a five-dollar note.

Many of the people at the stelling were of mixed race. Buffianda, they were called, people of mixed Amerindian, African, Chinese and sometimes East Indian bloods. Sugar Plum was mixed in this way, Challu reflected, as she came to tell them that a motor-boat was waiting to take them up to Good Shepherd Square, Upper Barima River, where she lived.

The boat, an Amerindian boy at its helm, was quick, even though it was loaded high with fish-cans and groceries. They passed the confluence of the Aruka, Barima and Kaituma Rivers before Challu had finished eating a star-apple Reenee had given him, and, after forty minutes or so, the boat cut its speed and moored at Sugar Plum's landing.

Good Shepherd Square was a place of dreamy silence. The river was sprinkled with corials, the people in them glancing at the strangers before returning to their fishing, or to ferrying their farm produce across the river. Sugar Plum pointed out the little troolie-thatched building which was their church, and the dilapidated mud-and-wattle school.

That night Sugar Plum took Challu and Reenee to a dance in the benab of a man called Mr. Sampat. The dance was being held jointly in the honour of Sugar Plum's return and to reward his neighbours for completing cayap work on his farm.

In the benab, the two Tilley gas-lamps hanging from the roof provided just enough light for Challu to watch the women in their gaudy dresses waiting to be asked to dance, and the men, when the juke-box started, breaking off from drinking from a large oil drum of casiri, piawari and tonic, to choose their partners. Sometimes they chose their own wives, sometimes those of others. All this without any sign of conflict.

'Why you so quiet?' Reenee asked him.

'Nothing,' he said curtly.

'You don't know to dance?'

'No.'

'Then let we go out on the river, rowing.'

It was a cloudy night, a slight hiss of rain in the distance, but the moon in the tiger-skin sky picked out every object in its glow. A man in a drifting corial was singing, 'Kumbaya… O, me Lord, Kumbaya', a jumbie bird cried and, deeper inland, the baboons howled.

'I like it here,' Reenee said. She was at the stern, dipping and pulling her oar. 'I is the queen of this night. The people here call me Princess. They don't know I is a prostitute.'

The rain in the distance began to hiss louder. The clouds thickened and drifted with the wind.

'We is in Hanaida Creek,' Reenee said. 'Five mile away from home. And the rain coming.'

The rain came with lightning flashing in swift, jagged forks. The moon disappeared with the stars and the punier sounds of the night yielded to the might of the downpour. Reenee and Challu laughed together as the pellets of rain exploded on their faces.

When they reached Sugar Plum's landing, her father, Ezekial Jerome, was there, a torchlight in his hand, looking out for them. He was a solemn-looking man, white-haired, his face contoured with wrinkles. He did not know his daughter was a prostitute, but often boasted to the river-folks that she was working at a Government Office as a stenographer and earning a big salary.

'I give Ena plenty education,' he would say proudly. 'She is now a big thing in this country. Doing such a big work to make people skin them eye and wonder.'

Sugar Plum had been one of the brighter girls at Barima River. When she won a place at a High School in Georgetown, Mr Jerome sent her to stay with one of his cousins in Sussex Street, Charlestown, so that she could attend school. Unfortunately, the cousin's two sons gave Sugar Plum quite a different kind of education, introducing her to drugs and the rewards to be had for offering them sex. Discos, fashionable dresses and flattering attention became much more interesting than attending school.

Before long they persuaded her to pose for pornographic photographs, and it was when she graduated from acting in oral sex scenes to performing live with animals that she fell into the hands of the Government Intelligence Service — and thence into the jaws of the Belmonte Hotel.

But happy in his innocence, Mr Jerome greeted Reenee and Challu with a smile. 'You must not go out like that in the rain, Princess,' he admonished, and took them inside.

Inside the cosy house, protected from the rain by its

roof of troolie thatch and from flood by its strong
simirupa pillars, Challu and Reenee sat in the nibbi chairs
drying themselves.

'You must eat something,' Mr Jerome said. 'There is
fry plantain with coffee on the table.'

As Reenee saw Challu's clumsiness in drying himself,
she brought him a cup of coffee and touched his head.

'You hair ain't dry properly. I going to bring a better
towel for you.' She brought the towel and began drying
his hair tenderly, her breathing laboured over him in the
rain and thunder. Challu shivered as a sudden flash of
lightning lit up the room.

'You look cold,' she told him. 'Come by the fire side.'

Challu joined her on the straw mat she had spread in
front of the fire packed with blazing wild mangrove logs.
They sat watching the dancing shadows and the lantern
swaying in the draught.

Reenee's hair was damp and loose, the wet tresses roll-
ing down her neck to her shoulders, her damp dress still
clinging to her body. For Challu she was truly the queen
of this wet, wild night.

She sipped her coffee and looked at him. She longed to
touch him, but sensed it was too soon to probe his silence.

'Want more coffee?' she asked.

'No.'

'What you want?'

'High wine.'

She poured for him and he drank until he had finished
almost half a bottle.

'Want to go to bed?'

'No.'

'What you want?'

'I like the fire.'

They sat together listening to the sudden squalls of wind and the crash as a palm tree fell to the ground. Reenee heard the rain hissing in ecstasy at the thrust of the wind. She could not hold back any longer, and inched her hand, crab-like, along the floor until it met his, her heart bounding with uncertainty. His hand tightened against hers and she felt a quiver of pleasure. Then her arms moved with a will of their own to fall tenderly around his shoulders. She sensed his need and drew towards him in obedience to her desire. She kissed him and he responded to the moistness of her lips and pressed gently on her breasts and kissed her once, kissed her many times, until she longed for him. He undressed her and entered her so that she flared like the fire. She felt him deep and sincere, meaningful and strong. He found her and then she was lost to the world like the old man singing dreamily on the drifting river.

When they came to themselves again, Challu noticed marks on her skin.

'What's that?'

She didn't reply at once.

'My husband use to beat me.'

He looked at her with a mixture of pity and disquiet but said nothing.

He took her to her room and they made love again. She

wept. She had never before met a man of such deep passion. 'You make me feel good.' she whispered. 'I use to
hate all men. They never make me feel the way you do.'
Challu said nothing. He had drained his flesh and his feelings into her. She absorbed him and he slept away.

Morning came. The storm was over. The river was
silent and placid as ever. Light gusts of wind were blowing and the air smelt fresh.

Reenee got up and opened the window, shading her
eyes from the sun burning the foliage oozing moisture
from last night's showers. Challu was still dozing. Reenee
looked at him and shivered with desire. He was sturdy
with disciplined muscles, dark-complexioned with a
neatly-carved face. She stooped and kissed him. He was
the crest of every inspiration the morning offered.

Sugar Plum rapped on the door.

'Coming!' Reenee shouted, throwing a blanket over
Challu.

'Why you leave the dance last night?'

'I been out in the river.'

'You enjoy it?'

'It been really good.'

'Come drink some coffee.'

Reenee went outside and fixed the coffee. She came
back and woke Challu. He opened his eyes, not sure
where he was. The smell of high wine was still pungent
on him, but when it dawned on him that he was not in
Donkey Bugle, he flung aside the blanket covering him,
only to pull it back when he discovered he was naked.

'I love you,' Reenee told him as she proffered the coffee.

He looked at her dubiously and did not stretch his hand to take it.

'Drink it,' she persisted, smiling.

He took it and sipped.

'You is sweet like the river,' she said. 'You make me the queen of the night.'

She dragged him out of the room and to the landing where the tide was right up to the ghat-steps, a thin mist rising above the chocolate-hued river.

'Let we swim across,' Reenee challenged.

Across was about a hundred yards to another landing. There were two Amerindian children standing there, gazing at them with curious eyes.

Challu plunged first and swam on until he reached across. Reenee made a gentle splash after him and swam with slow, long arms. When she reached Challu she was breathless. He helped her up to the landing.

'I never feel happy like this before,' she said. 'You make me feel like a complete woman.'

He kissed her lightly on the cheek.

'I feel like being with you here forever,' she continued. 'Forever.'

Challu smiled.

The next morning, before daybreak, they left Good Shepherd Square for Arukami with Sugar Plum and her father.

The boat quickly made it out of Barima River and

entered the Aruka River, flitting past droning coffee-mills, smoking benabs and burnt acreages of chopped-down cookrit and mangrove trees, where later young corn and ground-provisions would sprout. They passed Kumaka Stelling, deserted and sullen. Today was not a business day. Only a Buffianda girl was there, dipping her toes in the river and pumping a finger between her closed palm in an obscene gesture of ridicule.

Soon, Hosororo reared in splendour from the Aruka River, trees and a sprinkle of houses sleeping against its rust-brown slopes.

'I like it here; is so quiet,' Reenee told Challu.

'It looks as though earth and heaven meet here,' he said. 'You have real peace here.'

'Things is good up here. You can pick anything from the trees and eat. Fruit plentiful.'

'Why don't you come and live here?'

She lowered her eyes, close to tears. 'I have two children, I can't bring them here, wish though I could.'

Ten minutes later, Blue Mountain Hill came into view.

'When I die, I like my soul to live there,' Reenee said.

Challu smiled. 'Who lives there never dies.'

When they reached the mouth of the Coriabo river they had to stop to remove the trunk of a manikole tree that blocked their passage. Half-an-hour later though, they were at the foot of Arukamai hill. A fat Amerindian girl came to welcome them. Challu could not help noticing that her face was marred by chicken-pox scars and she wore dentures. She was Leona, Sugar Plum's uncle's woman.

'Your uncle tell me you coming,' she said.

She took them up to the school, where she was the only teacher. Inside the school, amidst scattered books and shreds of cassava bread and cookrit seeds, Reenee was struck by a vivid sketch of an angry cat on the blackboard. Leona's five Amerindian pupils were trying hard to copy it.

'They can't spell cat,' Leona said. 'So I draw it for them to learn.'

A large rat scuttled across the roof and a troolie branch fell on one of the children. She screamed in panic and Leona rushed to her and cuddled her until she hushed.

'Don't worry about that,' she told them. 'Nobody care what happens here. I is Headmistress, staff and sometimes pupil. Only five children come here. And they come only three times a week.'

She took them into her troolie-thatched house. It was no less neglected than the school. A rancid odour of long unwashed dishes burnt the nostrils.

They ate boiled corn and cassava bread with the pepper-pot she gave them. Then she offered them piawari and tonic, but Challu preferred his high wine. The women drank the piawari and danced to rock music from a battered tape-recorder.

They danced deep into midnight and when, finally, the music stopped, the moon was high and a wind blowing in the trees brought the distant sounds of the jungle. Reenee remembered last night and felt the urge of love.

She found Challu peering into the empty stillness of the

moon-blanched river. 'No-one live here except Leona,'
she said. 'Do you think she is happy?'

'I like the solitude,' he said. 'Man's future is here.'

Reenee did not understand, but she was growing accustomed to his philosophical excursions. On impulse she
flashed her hand in the water and let the spray splash into
him.

'What you do that for?' Challu's eyes were wide as he
swabbed the water from his face.

'I like to make a joke with you.'

He took her uphill under a balata tree in the graveyard
where camoudies and yellow-tails coiled amongst the
crosses of rock-mound tombs.

'Those snakes must be jumbies,' Reenee said, pointing,
but she was not afraid, even though the serpentine chill
mingled with the sounds of the night, of birds and
baboons, and with the sudden, piercing cry of an Amerindian hunter. Instead, in quiet trust, she lay with him on
the soft rug of dry leaves and gave him her flesh.

'Here is Heaven,' she told him, staring at the moon fil-
tering through the branches. 'But Heaven stay with me
for a short time only and then go away forever.'

'Why?'

'My past is dirty.'

'What is your past?'

'I don't like to tell.'

'I would like to hear.'

'I come from a big family,' she began waveringly.
'Twelve children of us all. My father was a cane-cutter.

Not a good father. He use to drink hard and beat my mother. She take me out from High School and put me to work because things been bad at home. There been a lot of young brothers and sisters to feed, so I had to give up a little of my ownself and think about them.

'I been working as a typist/clerk at a real estate place. The manager was a wicked man. He rape me and tell me be quiet or else I lose my job. I think of my mother. I think of my brothers and sisters. They are hungry. So I give in to the man. And he begin to abuse me openly in the same way and boast to the other men that I is he woman, a young girl like me. I been fifteen then. A time come when the whole place get to know about it and my parents too. But my father didn't care.

'My mother decide to marry me off to any man that come my way. So, she take me to Enmore at my aunt and ask she to find somebody to marry me. She find me a man and we married, but the money he get for work he use to drink it out. So I had to find a job. I begin work as a sales-girl at a store. My husband didn't like it. He start becoming jealous and begin to beat me, accusing me of having affairs with the men working there. I couldn't bear the licks from he. So I take my children and get away to my mother. My husband don't know where my parents live. So that was good for me.

'Then I find a job as an accounts clerk at a Government Office. That was where Boss Man come and trick me. He come and fool me that he going to give me a big job at a posh hotel. Then he take me to Belmonte Hotel and give me a strong dose of cocaine in a glass of coca-cola. I lost my senses and he raped me. Each day after that, for a whole month, he did the same thing. When I do catch myself, I find I was like the other girls — hooked to the Belmonte Hotel.'

Her face was wet with tears and Challu tried to console her. But she wept more. The snakes on the crosses were the resurgence of her past. They were jumbies that could still challenge her chance of future happiness.

The next day they went to Mabaruma, the principal administrative and commercial centre of North West District. It was a place where one could live, with a school and a hospital.

'I never know there use to be such a big hospital here,' Reenee said.

Challu looked up at her, puzzled by the excitement in her voice. 'How you come to that?'

'I thinking about my son.'

'Your son?'

'He sick. And I can bring he here. Here nice to live.'

Mabaruma was indeed beautiful, standing on a hill that rose from Kumaka and merged with the hilly range of Hosororo, Horse Hill, Tobago and Tiger Hill. It was reached by a road winding up through rocks set like teeth in the red loam and lined by rows of well-spaced, rubber trees. It was warm by day and cool at night. The inhabitants, it seemed, worked hard during the day and drank out their savings at night at a disco at the extreme western end of the settlement. It was there that Challu spent the night with Mr Jerome and the women.

The following morning he and Reenee visited Sebai. Challu liked the undulating sprawl of white sand and the occasional troolie-thatched huts on the banks of the river which crawled cool under its arcade of slanting manikole trees. The river was shallow enough to wade across. Challu splashed and floundered in it and Reenee plunged after, frolicking with the children who were swimming there.

'Do you like children?' Reenee asked.

This caught Challu off guard. Slowly, a cold impassive look came over his face and he didn't reply.

That night he did not make love to her.

3

They returned the following Thursday and Challu went straight back to Donkey Bugle.

He rapped on the door. Boras opened up.

'Where you been whole week, man?'

Challu ignored the question.

'What you cook?'

'Ochro and rice.'

He noticed a make-shift screen of jute-bags curtaining off the kitchen from the corner where they slept.

'Why you put that down there for?'

'Florrie behind there sleeping.'

'Oh,' Challu grunted, and went to the pot for food. He sat on the floor with knees drawn up and began eating.

From behind the curtain came the sound of shuffling feet, the rustling of a skirt and jingling of bracelets. Florrie emerged, arms folded under her breasts. When she saw Challu she checked back in surprise.

'Is that you, Challu?'

'What you doing here?' he asked, not looking up.

'I going to marry Boras.'

Challu still did not look at her. 'How is Shaldheim?' he

at last managed to ask.

'Not good. You father getting mad.'

Challu stiffened. The pain, which had dulled over the past week, returned with choking insistence. There could be no forgetting.

His father was an influential lawyer and businessman on Leguan Island. Challu's grandfather had settled there as an indentured labourer at the end of the nineteenth century. After completing his indentureship, he began purchasing land and cattle bit by bit from his savings. Over ten parsimonious years he bought the Shaldheim Estate and planted rice on it. When he died, he left Challu's father a prodigious inheritance of cash, jewellery, land and cattle.

Challu's father was just as ambitious. He read law in London, came back and expanded the estate. He opened several spirit and grocery shops and operated a large rice-mill. With affluence came power and an overbearing arrogance. He screwed up his nose at the impoverished villagers and shamelessly exploited them, neglecting his own wife and demanding pleasure from their helpless women.

'You are the queen of my home,' he would try to whee-dle his wife. 'Your freedom is here, in this house. The outside world is bad. You must not go there.'

His wife took this quietly, sometimes with a stifled sob, sometimes a wry smile but did not revolt. She dutifully gave him his conjugal rights whenever he demanded, and bore him five sons, four of whom became lawyers like their father. Challu was the last born. He could never reconcile himself to his father's ways.

'I'm not going to become a lawyer,' he told his father one day, 'if it means becoming like you.'

His father shook with disbelief, gathered himself and reared and seethed like a provoked kamakari snake. He threw Challu out of the family, forbidding him to set foot anywhere on the estate.

At first Challu was devastated by his father's action, but gradually he pulled himself together and adapted to his new situation with the conviction that it was better to live in honest poverty than be like his father and stink with guilt.

He went to the north of the island and lived with the villagers there. He worked in the fields with them and ate their simple meals. He shared in their pleasures of water-play and chowtal at Phagwah; greasy pole, donkey race, carols and masquerade at Christmas; fairs and fire-crackers at Diwali; gymkhana, regatta and kite-flying at Easter. He was often amazed at how generous the villagers could be, even though they were pressured by need, in luminous contrast to the dark ego of his father.

It was at Conversation Pond that he met Sareeta, a rice-farmer's daughter. She often went there to gather dried wood as fuel for the fireside. When she saw Challu monkey-slinging on a gargara limb for berries, she cried out in alarm: 'Watch yourself! Down there in the pond have alligator.'

Conversation Pond was where the villagers washed,

bathed and fetched water for cooking and drinking; a place for gossip and discussion of communal issues. It was also a place coloured with the myths of its past, of Dutch spirits manifesting as alligators, a place full of mystery.

Challu sprang down from the tree with a purple bunch of gargara berries. He gave some to Sareeta and, under the dappling sun-and-shade of a gargara tree, they sat and ate the berries, throwing the seeds to the alligators which surfaced from time to time.

From that day, they contrived to meet. Challu picked them berries and together they talked about the mystery of the pond. Sometimes they dug for old Dutch bottles and caked bricks and tried to find out how old they were. From the ruins of the sugar mill they tried to imagine how it had once been, and what cruelties had happened there. They talked about themselves, about their secret feelings, and tenderness grew into admiration and seasoned into love.

A month later, they dared all conventions and got married. It was a happy marriage. They laughed together. They tended the cows together and milked them and played with their calves. They caught hassars in their nests in the mucka-mucka trenches. They joined the farmers in their donkey-carts and ate the mangoes and star-apples that they brought from their farms. They caught lizards and played with them and roamed the jamoon groves and bathed in the river when the tide came up.

After a spell of drought came the rain. It soaked the parched grass and flooded the fields that had been languishing for lack of water. Now came the season of monkey-apples which ripened, fell and covered the mid-walks and canals with a thick yellow rug and filled the air with fragrance.

Challu and Sareeta went out with their girgiras to collect them, choosing the best from the bizee-bizee canals that hemmed in the fields deeper inland. They caught yarrows and houries that the rains had brought and joined the other villagers in taking patwas, sun-fish and snooks from the mud-beds of the shallower trenches. Everywhere was specked with the arched backs of the villagers. It was a festival of abundance. The rains had brought gaiety, the fertility of life.

On one of the mid-walks, Sareeta found a ewe and its newly-born milk-white lamb. She picked up the lamb and cuddled it as she would an infant. Challu saw a film of tears in her eyes.

'What is it?'

'Me like it,' she said shyly of the lamb.

She hesitated.

'Me getting baby.'

Challu's heart leapt with joy. And in this blast of pleasure, all that he could do was to lift his wife up in his arms and kiss her.

Four months later, the smell of ripening paddy began to waft in the air. The rice-fields had changed from dark green to yellow and then into a sea of billowing gold. Before dawn, bullock carts trundled up and down the road with the whack of urging whiplashes from the driver, and then, before the moon had died, the sudden deafening roar of the rice-mill came and drowned every other feeble sound. This awakened the rice-cutters and they marched out with their grass-knives to the rice-fields. Then the paddy was reaped and the sheaves bundled and taken to the karians to be threshed by bullocks or tractors.

The pyramids of paddy sheaves had to be watched. Thieves and arsonists rampaged at night. One lapse in the vigil could result in a whole crop ruined. So, Challu and Sareeta would go to watch their crops at night, lying on the stacked sheaves and staring out over the fields hedged with black-sage and goat-thorn brush.

'I love children, Sareeta,' Challu said one night.

She buried her face shyly in the straw.

'I want a son,' he continued. 'I want a son to come with me to the fields.'

She giggled and threw paddy grains in his shirt. 'If you want a son, take the sun in the sky.'

He took off his shirt and shook out the bristly grains from it and then wrapped her with it and held her to him for a moment. 'My son would help me keep watch at night,' he said. 'He would help me distribute the beeyas to the planters and scold the women when they don't do their task right.'

The father-to-be lay and built deeper dreams — a hammock for the baby-boy and milk for him from the best cow. 'I will take him to pick lokus when he starts to walk and to cut bamboo to make pens for the cows. You know how much I like lokus. In the bamboo we going to catch birds and iguanas,' Challu said.

Sareeta stuck out her tongue at him and screwed his nose. 'You dreaming mad things in you head.'

The child inside her began to ripen like the fields. Each day Challu looked at her with tense expectation.

Then one day he took her to the doctor. 'It's going to be a difficult delivery,' the doctor told him. 'It might need a caesarean.'

Challu grew pale. The question was money.

The following week Sareeta began to develop labour pains. Challu took her to the hospital and the doctor admitted her, though Challu had no money to lodge as an advance. He pleaded with the administrator that he would come back with the money — ten thousand dollars. The administrator shook his head and told him coldly that the advance was necessary.

He sought money from the villagers. They had none. The news reached his mother.

'Give he some money, Sam,' she exhorted Challu's father. 'He wife dying.'

Challu's father glared at her. 'Let her die. Women like that have no place in the world.'

Challu panicked. He had to find the money. His wife might deliver before noon the next day. There was only one way.

He entered his father's estate from behind the network
of bundarie trees that fortified the sea-dam against the
river and sat in the sun-and-shade of the large six-o-clock
tree that overlooked the stretch of river between the island
and the West Coast.

He watched the black smoke rising from the two sugar
mills on the West Coast and the derrick rising and falling
in the spree of the sun. His attention was caught by two
fishing boats in the steady dip-and-rise of the river, then
by the island, knobbed in a thick mane of mangrove and
courida trees, sticking out a haughty tongue at the Atlantic. This was a promontory of creamy sand known as
Dauntless, after the name of a cargo boat which had been
wrecked there over a century ago. There, in August of
each year, the full moon brought out hordes of crabs from
the sea to march from the site of the wreck.

Challu's mind wandered there in desperation. He and
his son would go there to catch crabs and bring them
home for his wife to boil in coconut milk. Then they
would sit under the baragat tree with the other villagers in
the moonlight and eat the crabs and talk Nancy stories
about Buroo Tiger and Buroo Goat.

He waited until midnight. It was a dark night. No
moon. Only stars. He waited until every current of life
had subsided, until the men left the fowl-cock tree where
they gambled at cards. He picked his course away from
the busy main road and began to force his way through
the hedge of kamawari thorns that bordered the troolie-
thatched houses where jug lamps were flickering in the

windows. In the dark, the spikes of the thorns tore his skin, but his will urged him on and he at last reached the gyama-cherry grove where the ground opened out into soft bahayma grass in front of a huge tamarind tree.

The tamarind tree was a childhood rendezvous where he had played cowboy and cockadillo. The canal from which it rose was now silted up and bristling with mucka-mucka, beezee-beezee and wild eddoes. Challu and the other boys had once swum in its coffee-coloured water and played cuffum and ducks-and-drakes and plucked the kamal-gatha lotus that grew on its parapets and eaten the nuts from its ovaries.

He sat under the tamarind tree, on the octopus spread of its roots, and he opened the book of his past, turning page after page slowly, each page filling him with pain, each stab of pain with the impulse to revenge. He looked to where the pillared coconut trees rose dimly in the shroud of the night, to the large bungalow which stood like a peeved monster between the fronds of a genip tree. This was where he had been born. There his mother had cuddled him and wept in stifled anguish. There he had heard the screams of women raped by his father. There he had seen his father concoct his crooked accounts to cheat the poor farmers.

Hate seized him. He wanted to explode, but a sense of his immediate purpose held him back: his wife, his child. He stole across to the genip tree that grew by the wallaba fence and paused there, thinking about his next move. In the rising wind, a thick flurry of branches brushed against the south-eastern windows of the bungalow, where a Pet-romax gas lamp was burning. He had often entered the house through this window, by monkey-slinging on one of the branches of the genip. Tonight he would do this again, though the branches might whir and cackle and attract attention.

As soon as he was in the house he knew that no one was at home. All the side windows were shuttered, though the ones facing the main road were left open — to deceive passers-by. The back window through which he had entered was often inadvertently left open. To finish the illusion of occupation, a gas lamp had been put on an iron table in the dining room, with no flammable materials within reach of the flames. They must have gone to the October Fair in Maryville, Challu thought.

Something crashed to the ground. Challu jumped back, breaking into sweat. He breathed a sigh of relief when he saw that it was his father's portrait which had fallen from the wall. His panic subsided and a deeper hate seized him. He ground his heal into the glass until the canvas was shredded. He kicked the door to his father's room. It was locked. He kicked again, harder. It flew open. He entered and stood there for a moment in a turmoil of thought.

Then in one swift motion he broke his pause and dragged out the wallaba-handled axe that lay under the bed. He held the axe over his head and in a gust of fury brought it down in crashing blows on the mahogany safe until it sagged into fragments. His fury subsiding, he let the axe slip from his hand. He gazed at the wreck on the floor. Was sin for sin wrong? Was it indeed a sin if it was done to earn a virtue? He was here for his wife and unborn child. Could that be wrong?

He thrust his hand into the shards of the safe and took out a canvas bag, his father's money bag. Then he picked up the gas lamp, swirled it over his head and flung it on the bed. With an ooze of kerosene and gas from the pump, it exploded and the mattress blazed into flames. He did not look back. He stole through the window and disappeared into the night.

Villagers broke out from every direction with cries of alarm, silhouette shapes running and panting with buckets and saucepans to fight the fire. The house was now engulfed in tongues of flame which licked the sky and everywhere the crowd gathered, marking the jagged periphery of the heat and the glow. The bucket brigade was a feeble combatant as the pitchpine and decades of paint made eager fuel for the blaze. Before dawn the building slumped to a charred skeleton, smoking stubbornly from the corrugated zinc which was still smouldering.

By dawn Challu was already on the steamer at the stelling. Hints of the disaster hung palpably in the dark scuds of smoke drifting in the air between the curve where the tower of St Peter's Church peeped through the silk-cotton trees and the neck of the land plunged into the river towards the Atlantic. Challu felt a deep inner pain, a pain that became sharper as the steamer piped its hollow signal and began to head off towards the Parika shore, as he saw the outline of the island and the promontory of Dauntless where he and his son would go to catch crabs.

When he reached the hospital, a cold feeling overwhelmed him. The nurses' faces were glum. A few patients who knew him gazed at him round-eyed, wondering if he knew. The porter hastily wheeled his stretcher away and did not give his usual friendly smile. The ward doctor shot him a cursory look and darted into his office. A patched labaria hissed and struck.

'Sorry, Mr Challu,' the ward sister said to him. 'The good Lord has done his best.'

The labaria hissed in the broil of the river and the alligators in Conversation Pond snapped their jaws.

'My son?' he asked, sweat pouring off his face. 'He, too?'

'Yes.'

Challu sat and ate the ochro and rice. 'My mother,' he asked Florrie, 'how is she?'

'She not been too well since the house burn down.'

'And what is my father doing?'

'He say he know who burn down the house. But he don't want to talk. The police looking for the man everywhere and questioning a lot of people.'

That same day, in the blinding glare of noon, Challu took Reenee to the La Repentir cemetery. They followed Sussex Street to reach the back entrance where columned coconut trees leaned over the trench that followed the street. The trees were yellow and wilting with the constant flooding, and the shells of water-ravaged coconuts were strewn here and there. Thieves were at work here too. A dismantled tomb revealed that they were robbing the dead as well as the living, of everything, even their caskets.

Challu and Reenee went through the broken gate and followed the mid-walk that cut through the cemetery from south to north. They paused where a flutter of palm trees soared and brushed against the sky. Challu leant against the serrated bark of a palm and gazed over the tombs which lay before them like a miniature city.

4

Relationships began to crack and crumble at Belmonte Hotel. It started with Boss Man's wife.

'I see Mistress with a man in a fancy car,' Tiger Cat told Boss Man.

Boss Man pretended a lack of interest. 'Oh she going around with me lawyer for business. We planning to open a posh restaurant in Regent Street.'

'But they been hugging up one another in the car,' Tiger Cat persisted.

'They just making friendly joke.'

'You call that joke when they been kissing-up and their mouth paste-up together like when two dog fasten?'

'You lie,' Boss Man said disbelievingly.

'I lie?'

'Then I don't care,' he said. 'I love Reenee.'

Tiger Cat laughed aloud. 'You ain't know Reenee going round with a man coming here every night?'

'What! I don't believe that.'

'Then you is a stupid big man.'

Boss Man hitched up his trousers and rushed upstairs to Reenee's room. She was putting on her make-up.

'So, you turn big, now?' he screamed. 'You kicking me and taking another man?'

'I never been you woman,' she said quietly, without looking at him, glossing her lips with lipstick.

'Is I bring you here and make you somebody.'

She pressed her lips deeper with the lipstick.

'You make me into a good prostitute.'

'You is not a prostitute. You is me woman.'

'You bring me here by brute force.'

'But I have you good. I giving you everything you want.'

'What you mean — money?' She looked at him askance.

'Money, food, clothes — everything you want.'

'You not giving me respect, though.'

Knowing he could not penetrate her resolve, Boss Man fell back on his usual tone of plaintive retrospection.

'I had me bad days too, Reenee. I been to jail for eight years.'

'Who tell you to make counterfeit money?'

'I always want to become rich. My mother dead and left me on the street without a penny.'

He had been born in Enmore and grown up fatherless in Albouystown. His mother dead when she was ten years old, he had joined the vagrants on the streets, selling cigarettes and sweets and avoiding school. At twelve years of age, he found himself in a ring in Tiger Bay Alley and emerged a slick campaigner in pickpocketing and shoplifting. Later, he graduated to choking-and-robbing and, on his thirtieth birthday, he was commissioned head of a gang for armed robberies. He kicked down many doors, raped and murdered and escaped with booties of thousands of dollars in cash and jewellery.

Good fortune was obviously on his side. He was never caught. His gang looked upon him as an idol. But as his confidence grew so did his need to test his luck. Gambling became an obsession and fuelled the need for money. What could be more logical than to counterfeit it?

For a time all was success. He became the biggest promoter of show-business in the country: concerts in the city, nude-shows in hide-outs, fashion shows on selected lawns. Occasionally, too, he would even invite prestigious orchestras from overseas to bring a little high culture to the country. But his avarice caught him hands up, pants down. One day he took in a million dollars for banking. The bank clerk took the wads of notes and studied him suspiciously. Boss Man smelt that something was not right this morning. He put on his awkward smile and began pricking his gums with a tooth-pick. The clerk checked through the notes unhurriedly, drew his chair aside and leant across to speak to the woman beside him. She stared coldly at Boss Man, picked up her telephone and buzzed. A security guard came and arrested him. Half of the notes he had brought were counterfeit. He was charged, convicted and sentenced to eight years imprisonment.

Jail did nothing to quench his ambition. After his release, he built himself a luxurious house in Enmore, the place of his birth, bought a limousine and started operating a rush of low-class, short-time hotels in the city. Beautiful women quickly fell prey to his confidence and lavish spending, until, uncharacteristically, he allowed himself to be seduced and hurried into marriage.

Now he complained to Reenee, 'I is not satisfied with me wife. It me fault. I cause it on meself.'

She sucked her teeth and continued painting her lips.

'That is you business.'

'I want you as me wife.'

'No man, you don't hear what I saying.'

Boss Man erupted into a splutter of abuse so loud it drew Sugar Plum, Nice Gyal and Tiger Cat to the room.

'Why you quarrelling with she for?' Sugar Plum asked.

'Mind you own damn business,' Boss Man said. 'Reenee is me property.'

Nice Gyal whispered something in Sugar Plum's ear and looked at Tiger Cat, her eyes filled with laughter.

'You mean Tiger Cat is you property,' Sugar Plum said.

Tiger Cat slapped Sugar Plum in the face.

Enraged, Nice Gyal rushed forward and cracked his head with a bottle. Boss Man's face was drawn with terror at the sight of the spurting blood. 'Oh me gaad! Stop it!' he shouted.

But Tiger Cat pounced on Nice Gyal, crashed her to the floor and began pounding her face with his fist. Her hand dropped by chance on the fangs of the broken bottle. In terror she grasped it and began ripping at him wildly.

Tiger Cat screamed and hit her even harder. Nice Gyal
was unconscious before Boss Man managed to pull him
off.

That evening Boss Man went home a deeply disturbed
man. He became even more upset when some youths
threw stones at his limousine and called him 'whore-
house minister' as he drove through the Enmore Station
Road to his house. He ranted back at them, honked his
horn madly and called their mothers 'Kaka-sideline
queens'.

Here was his own past returning to pain him. Once he
had been one of these boisterous, lewd young men, a nui-
sance wherever they perched in hordes at every junction,
idling noisily at every hour, entertaining themselves by
hurling obscene taunts at passers-by. Was there no escape
from this past of communal lawlessness and plantation
backwardness, where everyone gossiped about the other
and pulled down those who tried to better themselves?

Boss Man lived at the end of the road, in seclusion from
the other buildings, in a two storeyed, glass-doored house
fenced in with steel spikes and hedged around with
trimmed hibiscus. It reared above the immediate buildings, overlooking the cluttered hovels of the squatting
area beyond which the Enmore factory smoked and
roared. His house was passed by the stream of cane-cutters on their way from the sugar factory to the field. Fre-
quently they stopped and shouted abuse at Boss Man's
wife and hurled stones and cane-joints at his dog, which

jumped back and forth barking in reproval. This brought out the neighbours onto their verandahs to add their jeers. Then they would hiss and break out into laughter.

This evening Boss Man found his wife in the front verandah, reading, not in the least affected by the cane-cutters.

'You is giving me blow,' he greeted her, still in the crude rage provoked by the young men on the road.

'What do you mean?' she asked softly.

She was well-spoken, coming from a middle-class family. She had attended Bishop's High School, had worked as a receptionist at the Pegasus Hotel and won a National Beauty Contest when she was eighteen.

'I mean you is giving me blow,' he repeated, scowling.

'Could you tell me who is the blow-man?'

'Mr Rudolph Gurwah.'

She tightened her lips and giggled. 'Gosh, Dun, isn't he our lawyer?' 'Dun' was her name for him.

'Yes, he is me lawyer,' Boss Man agreed. 'But lawyer must do lawyer work. Lawyer must not play around with people wife.'

'You must not believe what people say, Dun. They don't like to see us living so well.'

But this merely spurred him into a tantrum. He broke the chandelier lamp on the verandah and pitched his shoes outside. The neighbours clustered on their verandahs once again and strained their ears to hear. The little boys playing at the street corner dropped their pants and skinned their buttocks at him. Mothers roared in approval, and

fathers drew on their cigarettes and looked on indul-
gently.

Boss Man didn't care.

'Stop it, Dun,' his wife pleaded. 'The neighbours are
looking at us.'

'To hell with the neighbours', he screamed, and flung a
chair outside.

The women craned their necks out and choked in their
laughter.

'Let them look,' Boss Man screamed again. 'They eye
going to fall out piece-piece. This is man-and-wife story.'

He fumed and swore all night. His wife kept calm,
waited until the fury had burnt out, put on a strong French
perfume, inundated him with kisses and told him how
dearly she loved him.

When he woke up next morning he was a changed
man. Under the shower he began whistling cheerfully
and, when he came out for breakfast, he exhorted his wife
to meet Mr Gurwah to conclude the deal on the property
they were buying in Regent Street. But he warned: 'You
have to watch that Mr Gurwah. He is a lawyer, and
lawyer like to rob people.

Boss Man's wife met Gurwah at the Palatial Rendezvous on Camp Street, one of the A-grade restaurants in the
city.

'Dun knows about us,' she told him.

He sipped his whiskey and smiled at her.

'So, what about that?' he asked. 'You just playing a
game.'

Mr Gurwah was in his mid-thirties, tall and well-featured with a neatly-chiselled nose. He seemed on constant guard to prevent any display of emotion.

'Last night he behaved badly,' she said. 'He performed a regular circus for the neighbours.'

'You married him for a reason,' he reminded her, 'and you have to see it through.'

The waitress came and brought their order.

'But how long do I have to carry on like this?'

'It'll soon be over,' he reassured her as he unwrapped the knife and fork from the tissue paper and began tearing at the meat on his plate. Later they went to No Man's Land Hotel on the West Bank.

'Rudy,' she said, 'I'm scared.'

'Of what?' he asked, his mind wandering. 'Because you're on top of me?'

'Oh, no,' she said with mild irritation. 'I am scared of how it could end.'

'It's going to end good.'

'Stop it, Rudy. We're playing with trouble.'

For a moment his face darkened, then he smiled blandly.

'It's only a game for money,' he said, pressing a finger in the soft fabric of her skin.

'But you have to act quickly, Rudy,' she breathed, feeling a new flush of passion as the finger went deeper.

'More quickly then this?' he said and kissed her.

As they crossed the Demerara Harbour Bridge back to Georgetown, she asked him, 'How would you do it, love?'

'As I always do it,' he whispered in her ear.

She gave him a tiny pinch on the shoulder. 'This is a serious matter. You taking it too lightly.'

'Ah, don't get nervous. I'm arranging things with a man at my lumber yard.'

'It's over twenty million dollars in cash and assets.'

'You are a lovely woman. You have imagination and colour.'

When she arrived home Boss Man asked her, 'How is the deal?'

'Fine. When it comes to business, I have imagination and colour.'

'How much Alphonso selling for?'

'Only five million.'

'That good. We going to open the biggest restaurant in this city.'

Boss Man drove back to the Belmonte Hotel and broke the news to Tiger Cat. 'I going to buy the biggest restaurant in the city. Five million dollars.'

'That good,' Tiger Cat said, his head still bandaged from Nice Gyal's attentions. 'You have to buy tie-and-jacket for me. I going to be the chief waiter.'

It was then that Boss man noticed Challu in the corner. 'Is that the man?' he asked Tiger Cat under his breath.

Tiger Cat nodded.

'Then you know what to do?'

'I know, Boss. The boys of Donkey Bugle will settle him.'

This pleased Boss Man and he looked at Reenee behind the cashier's grille and thought how foolish she was. Reenee sensed his gaze but could not read his thoughts.

Challu drank till midnight. Just as he was leaving, a total power outage snapped the streets in darkness, save for where little generator plants droned. The noise of the traffic thinned out, but the roving dogs still barked and howled and the bands of men who prowled the streets were, as ever, out seeking prey or plunder. As ever, they passed Challu as if he was invisible.

He reached Donkey Bugle without incident, but when Boras opened the door to him, he was weeping.

'What happen?' Challu asked.

'Me wife should never have left me.'

Challu gave him a hard look. 'You want some good hammering in your backside.'

'Me wife left me for good and me can't talk.'

'What happen with Florrie?

'She is only a side-dish.'

'You playing the rass.'

'Me wife should never have left me. Me is a good-good husband.'

'So why she left you.'

'Me use to give she a little licks one-one time because me really love she.'

'You making love like when people playing bat-and-ball.'

Boras ignored him. 'Me love me children too.'

Challu could not bear it. 'Go find your damn children.'

'Where me going to find them?'

'In my ass.'

They quarrelled on through the night until sleep over-took them. When morning broke, Boras said, 'Me cook-ing sweet-sweet fowl curry for you today, yeh?'

5

Bad news came for Reenee. Her father had died. For half-a-day she sat at a table, pulling in her knees with her arms and weeping. All the women stayed away from their work and gathered around her, trying to comfort her. She did not want to go to the funeral, though; home had too many painful memories.

'You must go,' Nice Gyal insisted. 'It is you own father.'

Reenee buried her face between her thighs and wept more.

'And you going to get to see you children,' Sugar Plum added.

Reenee raised her head and looked at her. Whatever else home meant, she could not deny the urge to see her children. Even so, she insisted that Challu should go with her, and seeing her need, he did not refuse.

That same evening they set off to catch a taxi to Rosignol at the Berbice car park. As they passed Bath Settlement, Reenee craned her neck through the window and pointed to a derelict house, the paint on its walls patchy and fading, windows hanging loose, the front stairs collapsed, the ochre zinc roof rusting and clanking in the wind.

'I use to live there,' she said. 'My husband been cutting cane for Blairmont Estate.'

In the middle of the Berbice crossing, the steamer crawled against the tide, struggling even more in the mouth of the river where the Atlantic yawned, swelled and flowed from a blurred horizon. Challu gazed in turn at each shore, at the dense thickets of mangrove trees, at the wharves where schooners and smaller vessels berthed beside the factories and warehouses. On the west bank, beyond the dark belt of mangroves, his eye was caught by the chimney of the Blairmont Factory rising up into the purple sky.

'Are you sure your husband does not know where your parents live?' he asked.

'No,' she said. 'I never tell him.'

As they got closer to New Amsterdam, they began to pick out the haphazard cluster of buildings, the criss-crossing bumpy streets. Nearer still they heard the buzz of sawmills and saw the clouds of sawdust which powdered the whole area, and even before they landed they smelt the stink of the rat-infested market and the grimy mounds of refuse on the street corners.

Passing the beggars, the insane, the boisterous prosti-tutes busy seducing drunks, they joined a clanking, noisy Morris Oxford heading for Port Mourant. The driver, a greasy, grizzle-bearded man rambled on about God and charity until his taxi broke down on the bridge over the

Canje River; thereupon, he cursed God and all the prophets who had ever been born.

At Port Mourant, the market was crowded with thousands of people gathered in a steady drift of commerce: hucksters flaunting their goods and pronouncing their quality; buyers pleading for a better deal.

'My mother use to sell here sometimes,' Reenee told Challu. 'I use to help her.'

The taxi stopped at the bridge over a trench draining the flood water from the fields into the sea. They got out and followed the mud dam snaking along the trench into the canelands.

'That is the estate dispensary,' Reenee pointed out when they reached the junction of the mud dam and the cross-road. 'I use to go there part-time in the afternoon to study and learn the work. At that time I want to become a nurse.'

Further along the dam, they reached the temple, built India-style with three spires and a dome. A large peepal tree in the front yard towered above a margossa tree stuffed with jhandi flags.

Reenee stopped and looked in pained reverence.

'That is the siwala. The best in the world for me.'

Challu stood beside her in silence, moved by Reenee's evident feelings.

'It start with an old man,' she said, 'who been fasting for rain. Then he dead and the temple was built. Years and years ago.'

'Years and years ago,' the jhandis sang.

'Many great people was born here,' Reenee said. 'Their parents use to bring them here to pray.'

'Bring them here to pray,' the peepal tree sang.

'I use to pray here, too,' Reenee said, 'and think of the old man. But I never become what I dream for.'

They turned left into Ankerville Settlement, past the yards, each with their fluttering jhandis. Dust-powdered trees shrouded the cluttered houses and the sand–dirt streets that ran into yards, pit-latrines and ditches, where pigs and children rooted companionably in the mud.

They went into the yard of one of the houses. A girl of five came out to welcome them and Reenee kissed and hugged her excitedly. 'This is my daughter,' she told Challu.

Her mother came out, too, and told Reenee in moans of distress that her father was already buried. She was a thin woman, worn by stress and fatigue, her skin crumpled with age.

She explained to Reenee how her father had been drinking without restraint for a good whole month, not coming home for meals and rest, lying anywhere he fell — on the street corners, under a coconut tree, in dirty ditches or sometimes in the bottom-houses of folks who pitied him. One Saturday night when he'd been drinking bush rum at Ketten Dam, he'd lain on the parapet of the trench near the siwala, slept away, slipped into the trench and drowned.

Reenee wept bitterly. Good or bad, he'd been her

father. She could not hold back her grief. She agreed with Challu that next morning they would go to the Haswell cemetery where he was buried.

On their way, she pointed out to Challu the real estate office where she had worked. It was now abandoned and infested with wood ants, the front door and back stairs missing. Even now, the place filled her with revulsion. It had been here where her honour had first been taken. She was fifteen, full of dreams that she would become a real nurse, a professional like the ones working in the big hospitals. She prayed each day at the siwala, offering the gods fruits and flowers and performing arti before them. She fasted on Fridays and Sundays and on each auspicious day of the Hindu calendar. She helped in the cooking when there were festivals and pujas in the community. And she would attend Satsangh and sing bhajans. She had a beautiful voice and the priests and elders praised her and wished her well. They foretold she would make a chaste and dutiful wife like Anusuya.

But one morning, her boss, unable to resist the bloom of her body, her ripening hips and maturing breasts, could not contain himself any longer. He called her into his office and told her that she was working well. She held back her delight and smiled shyly, but she was sure now that the gods she had served were all pleased with her. She offered them even more fervent prayers and more splendid bunches of flowers.

The next morning he told her, 'You can come with me to New Amsterdam.'

She felt privileged to go with him. It was a warm day of motionless air during a long period of drought and failed crops. She remembered the pained faces and pot-bellied children along the way, wilting for want of food.

Her boss took her to an expensive hotel and bought her a soft drink.

'You are beautiful,' he told her. She smiled. She still did not understand.

But when he led her to a room with a bed, locked the door and told her he would increase her pay, understanding dawned.

'Don't be scared,' he said. 'Sit on the bed.'

He was a fat man in his fifties, his head balding, a tussle of greying hair at his temples. When he took off his clothes, the muscles on his chest sagged like the breasts of a lactating mother.

She sat on the bed, crossing and uncrossing her legs in a chill of realisation.

'You understand why you're here?'

'No.'

'You are here to do what all bosses like.'

She was filled with disgust. She did not want to take off her clothes, but her boss was impatient. He pulled her down on the bed and ripped off her underwear, ignoring her screams of terror and her pleading. In seconds she was naked and he plundered her.

After that he did what he liked with her. She relapsed into fits of cheerlessness; ambition and hope squeezed out of her. She no longer went to the siwala and prayed. She passed the singing jhandis, head-bent, guilt etched into her conscience.

They reached the cemetery where her father was buried beneath a brown mound of dirt with no wreaths on it. She dropped to her knees and took a handful of dirt and wrung it tightly.

'Pa, you leave me without a future and gone,' she wept in shuddering sobs. 'You never been thinking about me and the world.'

She wanted everything to weep with her: the white cranes pecking in the duck-weed canals, the goats nibbling leaves over the trench and the quarrelling kiskadees building nests in the trees.

'Now I have no strength to fight,' she screamed. 'You drink it all out.'

'You drink it all out,' sang the kiskadees, and their cry echoed and echoed past the sand reef, the grove of coconut trees and dissolved into the wrath of the sea.

That night Challu slept on a narrow child's board-bed in the hall. The bed stank of urine and was branny with tattered bedding, the bed-sheets unwashed and brown with dirt.

On the floor, beside the bed, the children cuddled tightly into each other, wrapped in sleep. One of them was moaning and writhing, his head, arms and legs moving in a taut rhythm of pain. This was Reenee's son who had been knocked down by a bicycle when he was a toddler and left handicapped. He was about seven years old now, but dwarfed by malnutrition and neglect.

Downstairs the men and women were keeping the thirteen-night wake, singing bhajans and kirtans amidst the rattling of dominoes. One of them sang about dharma, the personal, moral and social duties of a man. Challu sat up and studied the children in the dim lantern light. His heart raced like the estate water-pump which zik-zakked madly over on the other side of the race course. What is dharma, he asked himself, when a child is born and left to suffer in a misery made by others? What is dharma when the rich and privileged live in extravagance, abuse vulnerable women, turn terror on hungry children and give charity, not with the heart, but with cold hands. Then he heard a woman sing about karma, the divine law of action and reaction. She sang about how the rich and powerful must prosper from their past good lives; the poor suffering because of their sinful deeds. Challu twisted his lips in disgust. That was the danger with such mysticism, he thought, when a community misunderstood its past and refused to grow out of a social order of stench and squalor, greed and cowardice, exploitation and apathy.

6

When Challu got home to Donkey Bugle he found Boras
fighting with Florrie. The whole room was in disarray —
cups and plates, pots and pans strewn in a muddle on the
floor and Florrie's nose was bleeding.

'You take me for you wife?' Florrie yelled at him. 'You
get no right to beat me. Dog!'

Boras pounced upon her and hit her on the mouth. One
of her teeth flew out in a stream of blood. She bawled in
agony.

'You must learn to have one man,' Boras bawled.
'Woman like you does cause murder.'

'Why you ain't go and look for you wife and tell she
that?'

'You don't have me wife class,' he gritted his teeth. 'Me
wife don't pick fare.'

'You wife is a whore!'

Boras lunged towards her again and kicked her on the
leg. She screamed again and the man upstairs, who was
also beating his wife, laughed with pleasure.

Finally, Challu intervened. 'Boras stop it!'

Boras recoiled and mumbled a few incoherent curses.

Challu turned to Florrie. 'Florrie, get out!' She thought it wise to do so. Cursing, she bolted through the door and disappeared into the dark.

'Why you beat her so?' Challu asked.

'She taking man on me head.'

'She could report you to the police.'

'That is she problem. When she been taking me money, it been sweet.'

'But you shouldn't beat her. You have no business with her.'

'Business!' Boras exclaimed. 'Me been giving that whore two thousand dollar a week.'

Challu looked hard at him, 'You're going to get jailed.'

'For what?'

'For stealing.'

'Me is not a thief. The money me get is hard-earned money. Me boss heself does give me the money.'

'Your boss is stupid?'

'You call he stupid, eh?' Boras said. 'You call Mr Rudolph Gurwah stupid?'

Challu's heart bounded like a frightened deer.

'Rudolph Gurwah?' he whispered incredulously.

'Yes, Rudolph Gurwah,' Boras repeated. 'Me carrying out a mission for he. Me is he secret agent.'

From that day Challu spoke little and brooded long. He dreamt bad dreams and when he woke he saw ill omens in the clouds. He studied Boras carefully and tried to probe as subtly as he could, but couldn't get much from him. Though Boras drank hard and talked constantly about his wife, children and new-found fortunes, Challu could not tempt him into any indiscretion about his work for Rudolph Gurwah. Gurwah liked him for that.

'You are a good guy,' Mr Gurwah would tell him. 'You don't like to wag your tongue.'

Boras would glow at the compliment and say, 'Thank you, Boss.'

Boras was smart in other ways. When he had to visit Boss Man's wife, he did it with careful timing, ensuring that he would not confront Boss Man at his home. From a nearby beer-garden, he would take his stance, sipping a beer and spying on Boss Man's house. As soon as Boss Man passed in his car to town, he would walk carefully into his yard, wanting to suggest to the men and women staring down at him from their verandahs that he had every right to be there. He would fondle Boss Man's dog, which in time came to frolic around him when it sensed his arrival. This mystified the lookers-on, since the dog didn't like anyone in the neighbourhood. Amidst all of this, Boss Man's wife would emerge to receive him; Boras would smile broadly, exchange courtesies and go upstairs at her invitation. He would come down quickly, play with the dog and disappear out onto the main street. Though his business mystified everyone, the neighbours assumed, as they were intended to do, that Boras was one of Boss Man's men.

One evening Boras brought Boss Man's wife the message that Mr Gurwah wanted to meet her at the No Man's Land Hotel.

'Rudy,' she told him, 'I'm having weird dreams. I'm scared.'

They were in the room overlooking the Demerara River. The waves on the noon-gilded river looked like a crumpled sheet of foil flaming against the smoking skyline of Georgetown. The sight reminded Mr Gurwah of Leguan, but he stifled his musings and replied dryly: 'Nothing is going to happen, I'm sure.'

She kissed him, but he was still immersed in the river, watching a bow of sea-birds swooping and skimming and swooping up again over the water and finally soaring away into the sky.

'I love my island,' he told her.

'You have told me that a hundred times,' she said with an impatient gesture. 'You must forget it.'

'I can't forget the house I was born in,' he said reflectively. 'Now it's no more.'

'It's so sad.'

'I will treat fire with fire.'

'Rudy, you have to temper yourself down,' she said affectionately. 'Or everything else will fail.'

'Nothing will fail. I will find the culprit.'

She saw the growing desperation in his eyes and wanted to appease it. She took off his shirt and fondled the dark wisps of hair in the hollow of his chest. He hardly responded, but, when she took off her blouse and brushed him gently with her full breasts, he was awakened to a great rush of desire. She absorbed him deeply until she became breathless, and then satisfied.

When she arrived home, she found Boss Man at the dining-table, tearing at a chicken leg. 'I tell everybody that I buying the biggest restaurant in town,' he said excitedly, his mouth stuffed and guzzling.

She threw an arm around his shoulders and kissed him.

'You are the sweetest husband in the world.'

'I know that,' Boss Man said, stuffing a large slice of tomato in his mouth.

'And I love you dearly.'

'If you ain't love me, you won't cook good-good food like this for me.'

She smiled and picked up a curl of onion with a fork and thrust it into his already full mouth.

'Today is your forty-fifth birthday,' she said charmingly. 'Did you forget?'

'Oh yes. Oh yes,' he said, chewing vigorously and swallowing great lumps.

'I wanted to surprise you.'

Boss Man guffawed and a chunk of meat fell out of his mouth. 'You have a cake too?'

'Yes, I have a big one, with you made out of candy on the top.'

He guffawed again. 'Bring the cake. I like cake.'

'We have to light candles on it and you have to blow them out.'

'Bring the cake. Cake made to eat. Not to put candle on it.'

'No, Dun, don't do that,' she chided. 'The cake is to make a great day for you.'

'Great day when I hungry? Bring the damn cake, man. I like cake.'

She went and lit the candles on the cake and brought it. Boss Man blew out the candles and she sang 'Happy Birthday', clapping her hands.

Boss Man put his chicken away and embarked on the cake. He appraised it fondly, sliced off big chunks and ate hungrily.

'Oh no, Dun, you suppose to feed me the cake first and then I will feed you back.'

'Don't worry with all that nonsense. You have any more dishes?'

'I have omelette with cheese.'

'Bring it if it good to eat.'

She brought the omelette with cheese.

Boss Man looked at it and his face turned sour. 'You know I don't like fry-egg.'

He finished much of the cake and returned to the chicken.

'You want anything more?'

'I going to tell you just now. Let me finish off the chicken.'

'I feel happy to see you enjoy the food.'

'You must cook like this every day.'

When he had finished, he told her he was going to the hotel on urgent business.

'But I coming back just now,' he said. 'I coming back to eat...'

He couldn't remember the name of the dishes.

'Yogurt and pizza,' she helped him.

At the hotel, Challu was in his corner, silent, aloof, sipping his high wine. Boss Man's eyes fell upon him and he was stricken by a pang of hate. But when Challu returned his gaze, Boss Man pretended his attention was engaged elsewhere, loudly instructing the women to do their chores.

'How things going?' he asked Tiger Cat.

'All set tonight, Boss,' Tiger Cat whispered. 'The boys waiting for he tonight.'

That night Challu left, as he was accustomed to do, just before midnight. As ever the sounds of the traffic mingled with the howling and baying of the dogs. When he reached the High Bridge he slackened his pace to a mere dawdle and studied the prospect of the settlement before him. The lantern-post, with electric lamps on bent arms, reared up like Moon-Gazer. The solitary house near the cemetery looked like a huge casket sheltering corpses. The log on Miss Alice's roof looked like a mermaid, arms akimbo, gazing up into the sky. Then the whole settlement rolled like a large tidal wave, consuming everything in its path.

The Moon-Gazer loomed clearer now, head angled to the dull disc of the moon.

Challu felt a sharp quiver of apprehension, then alarm when the scream of a woman shredded the silence. A baby whimpered and a dog bayed in melancholy. The corpses pushed up the lid of the casket and dispersed in bizarre revelry. The mermaid rose and swam in the thin air of the moon, with slow, measured movements of her arms. Challu saw her coming towards him. Then she dealt him a sudden chop on the head, and several more after. He collapsed to the ground, the tidal wave swallowed him and he lost grip of his senses.

When he regained consciousness he found himself on a bed, Reenee sitting beside him, his body numb with pain and swaddled with bandages. Around him there were beds everywhere. At the foot of his bed, saline and blood-sacks hung from a stand. Then he saw the needles fastened in his forearm.

Reenee saw his dazed, inquiring eyes.

'You is in hospital.'

He tried to speak. Words could not come.

'Somebody chop you up last night. We find you on the road last night after a man see you and tell we.'

Challu wondered who was the man who had saved his life.

'The man know you well,' Reenee continued. 'He often come to the hotel to drink.'

He spent three weeks in hospital, Reenee bringing meals for him and doing his washing.

'Only God saved you,' a doctor told him. 'They hacked you like beef. One hundred and ten stitches.'

The bandages began coming off and Challu could now get a closer look at the wounds. He took two mirrors and looked at the back of his head. There were two one-inch lacerations in it. On his right shoulder was a two-inch long gash. Somebody had been trying to dismember him.

On the other shoulder were smaller gashes. Then his blood ran cold when he saw the long slice down his back. His assailant's purpose had been to slash him in halves.

The day before he was discharged, Reenee brought flowers and ice-cream.

'You look really good without high wine,' she smiled.

'I badly need a drink,' he protested.

'I don't want you to drink back.'

'Why?'

'You don't know why?'

'I don't know.'

'Because I love you.'

He paused and looked at her warmly. She saw the flood of feeling in his eyes and dropped on her knees and kissed him.

'I don't want people to kill you,' she said.

He shivered.

'Don't go back to the hotel,' she advised. 'Boss Man don't like you.'

She took him back to Nice Gyal's house at Non Pareil to recover from his wounds. By virtue of its position a mile and a half inland from the public road, Non Pareil had always been a place of sanctuary. Situated between Buxton and Enmore, with acres of pasture land to the north and west, in the 1960s it had been a place of refuge for political militants fleeing from British troops. In recent years a new housing scheme near the public road — mainly occupied by the ruling party's Afro-Guyanese supporters — had further isolated it. Though now a political and social backwater, it was an ideal place for Challu to lie low.

Nice Gyal's mother treated him with special care. She fed him chicken soup, inspected his wounds and insisted that he take his medication on time. No one was allowed to disturb his rest. The trampling, scuttling children would be hushed and marshalled out of the house to continue their police-and-thief game in the yard.

Reenee stayed with him and nursed him, too. They slept in one room and she told Nice Gyal's mother that he was her husband.

The wounds were healing quickly and Challu was now able to take brief strolls in the backyard where red-breasted robins where singing in the jamoon trees. Soon he had enough strength to go into the front street and play soft-ball with the little boys. The neighbours poked their heads through their windows and tried to figure out who he was. But no-one talked.

When Challu went home, he found Boras drunk, lying stretched full-length on the floor, lamenting over his wife and children.

'Where you been all these week?' he asked Challu.

'Nowhere,' Challu murmured.

'You look shine, man,' he said, propping himself up on his elbows. 'Like you been to Canada or what?'

Challu said nothing.

'Me complete me mission, man,' Boras told him. 'Me boss give me a lot of dollars.'

He fished out a thick wad of twenty dollar notes from his pocket and threw them in front of Challu who stared at them uncertainly. 'What kind of mission?' he asked.

'You don't know what kind of mission? Mission is like James Bond Mission.'

'Boras, tell me, what is this whole damn thing about? I must know.'

'You don't business with me. Me getting up in life. Like you jealous or what?'

'You'll go to jail.'

'Who going to jail? Me boss is the biggest lawyer in the world. But me wife and children should be around now,' Boras continued, 'to see how me get rich.'

Challu was not listening any more. He couldn't summon the energy to argue.

'Me invalid son,' Boras moaned. 'Me wife is a bad woman to separate me from me invalid son.'

The next day Reenee came to visit Challu. Her face was pale and distraught.

'What happen?' Challu asked. 'You look sick.'

She gave way to a deluge of frightened tears. 'Boss Man is dead,' she said. 'Bandits go to Enmore last night, kick down Boss Man' door, rob him of all the money he had home, shoot him dead and burn down his house with him inside.'

Challu felt a tidal wave of desperation rushing towards him. He bristled and sweated.

'You isn't well, eh?' Reenee asked, noticing the sweat.

'I'm fine,' he lied.

She placed a tender hand on his neck.

'You is sweating and having fever.'

'No, I am all right...'

A heavy banging on the door interrupted. It was Boras. He was drunk again, his clothing covered in dust and dirt. Challu opened the door. Boras staggered in. When his eyes landed on Reenee, he froze.

'Reenee!' he managed to cry.

She gulped down a flow of spittle and could say nothing.

'Reenee,' he said, 'you here?'

He began to weep and then turned to Challu. 'Friend, this is me wife.'

Challu became stone; then sweat began to fall from him in large, beading drops.

Boras fell to his knees before her. 'Reenee, where is me children?'

'Home.'

'Where is home?'

She did not answer.

'Reenee, me wrong you. Me use to beat you. Treat you bad.'

'You have to forget me,' she told him. 'Now I is a different woman.'

'No, Reenee, you can't do that. You is me wife. You have children for me.'

'Children? You never care about you children.'

'Who tell you so, Reenee?' he cried. 'Me love me two

children. How is Joey?'

'Joey is okay,' Reenee said. 'But he still ain't walking.'

Boras began to drum his chest with his hand, 'O, me gaad, me son really punishing! Me don't know what happen to me life.'

Challu could listen no more. The fever raged in his body and he grew dizzy and light-headed. He stumbled to the door and went outside for air.

Gurwah and Boss Man's wife met again at No Man's Land Hotel. It was a quiet morning with a harsh sun in an overcast sky; the waves on the river gleamed and blushed in the shadows of the passing clouds.

'Everything is over,' Gurwah said calmly.

She leaned forward and kissed him lightly on the cheek. 'I am scared, honey.'

'What for?' he asked.

'I am scared that the law will get to know we are involved.'

'I know how to handle that.'

'What about the man who set up the bandits to murder him and burn the house?'

'Boras? I'll take care of him.'

'I still scared, honey,' she said. What if they question me about why I was not at home?'

He kissed her. 'There's nothing to be scared about. The facts are like this: armed bandits were rampaging Enmore, broke into eight houses, burnt two, murdered one person and wounded others. This is a clear case of armed banditry. No suspicion can fall elsewhere.'

'You still haven't answered my question. What about me?'

'Why are you so frightened?' he said. 'It was your good luck that you weren't at home that night. Or else the bandits would have killed you. You went to spend a night with your mother. Didn't you?'

'I hope the police won't question me.'

'They won't.'

'Do the bandits know about us?'

'Of course not. Boras did a clean job. He gave the men half a million dollars to do the job. And they did a professional job and cleaned up the whole damn place.'

'I feel guilty about it.'

'For what? Dun was an armed bandit himself in his earlier days. He kicked down plenty of doors and murdered tens of innocent people. Look at what happened to him as just retribution.'

She looked unconvinced but said nothing.

The river now began to grow choppy. A strong trade wind was blowing. Flights of clucking birds winged their way westwards, accompanying the clouds that heralded rain. The sun weakened and cowered behind the clouds, softening the jagged outline of the city into a sombre haze.

'It didn't rain for a long time — two months,' she said.

'I like rain,' Gurwah replied. 'I used to relish it on my island. For me, it means abundance and strength.'

'I'd like to go to your island.'

'You'll love it,' he told her. 'It's a little diamond in the mouth of the river.'

The rain came down, rattling in tantrums on the corrugated zinc roof and the coconut trees in the yard began to sway in a frenzy.

'I love rain,' Gurwah said, looking out into the haze. 'I love to see the cows romp and jump in the rain. It speaks to me of fertility.'

'Doesn't it remind you of anything else?' she asked, her eyes filled with mischief.

He paused and smiled.

'Yes,' he said. 'Love.' And in the soporific music of the rain, he kissed her.

'All my brothers like rain,' Gurwah said. 'We are a family with a strong passion for rain. It awakens within us the deepest strain of love.'

'I would like to meet you family

'After we get married.'

She kissed him. 'How soon?'

'Very soon.'

'Darling, I'm eager for that day.'

'You have to wait a little.'

'Why?'

'I have something I must do.'

'What is it?'

'It's about my brother.'

'What with him?'

'A year ago he burnt our house down.'

'Gracious,' she exclaimed.

'I happen to know his whereabouts,' he said bitterly. 'A

woman called Florrie told me where he is.'

'What would you do if you find him?'

'I don't know.'

The next morning a fellow worker brought news to Challu that Boras had suffered a fatal accident at the lumber-yard — a plank had fallen from a huge stack of timber and cracked his skull.

Challu rushed to the lumber-yard and pressed through the crowd, hoping that the news was not true. Then he sagged in despair when he saw his friend lying in a pool of blood, skull splintered open, brain spattered.

He dropped on his knees and held the body tenderly, tears dropping from his eyes. Then the crowd thronged around him and he felt pairs of hands dropping hard on him and clenching his arms. When he looked up, he saw four armed policemen wrenching him up. They handcuffed him and told him that he was under arrest for arson.

Out of the crowd stepped Rudolph Gurwah. With gritted teeth, he slapped his brother's face.

'How do you do, Mr Challu Gurwah? For a whole year, for every moment of that time, I've burned for this moment.' Then he hit him again.

The policemen took Challu to a police station outside the capital. Its zinc roof was painted ochre, the walls white, though stained with rusty patches. Two flags were fluttering in the yard against the glint of a broken window — the National Golden Arrow Head and the Guyana Police Force Flag, under which two stray dogs were copulating. The compound, fenced around with wire-mesh and barbed wire trellised with baby sumootoo creepers and ban-caroilla vines, was littered with cigarette packs and dog droppings.

Challu sat in a green iron chair before a desk covered with grimy sheaves of paper. A burly plain-clothes officer stormed in with heavy, stomping boots. He fished out a coconut bun from his pocket, took a huge bite, chewed vigorously between missing front teeth and flung himself into a chair and surveyed Challu contemptuously.

'So you is the bad man who burn down his family's house.'

A police officer burst into the room and interrupted him. 'Sarge, Sarge, the man we bring in last night for bush-rum shit up in the cell.'

Sarge licked the gap of his missing teeth with his tongue and took another bite from his bun.

'Beat his ass and let him clean it up.'

He turned to Challu again.

'Yes, bad man, I want to hear the truth. Give me no hard card. We is friends.'

Challu did not respond; he sat, head bent.

A cockroach discovered the crumbs of the bun that had fallen on the floor. Sarge eyed it jealously. When it pushed its antennae out and began to nibble at the crumb, he raised his boot and dropped it upon it with sadistic triumph. 'I catch you, you sonuvabitch.'

Challu winced as Sarge's face opened into a smile.

'These cockroach.'

Sarge got up from the chair and belched. 'Come with me,' he motioned.

Challu followed him.

'Have you ever tasted what you eat?' Sarge asked sweetly as they walked up the steps.

Challu did not answer. Sarge looked at him over his shoulder and winked cheerfully.

As soon as they entered the corridor, the stench of the toilets hit them. A rat scuttled across. Sarge pulled a face. 'Rats! This country is full of rats.'

He stopped and winked again at Challu. 'Our duty is to make people say the truth and nothing but the truth.' He wiped the crumbs from his mouth, then tightened his hand into a fist, and swung a heavy thudding blow into Challu's abdomen. He groaned and buckled to the ground. Then Sarge lifted his boot, scraped backwards on the cigarette ends on the floor and drove forwards in a flashing kick to Challu's head.

Blood began to pour from Challu's head. Sarge bent down, grabbed his shirt caressingly, and pulled him up with a show of gentle care. 'Come on, bad-man, I told you we is friends. Talk and make this game easy.'

Challu still would not talk.

Sarge shrugged his shoulders 'Then you don't want to be my friend. So shall it be.'

He took Challu to the unwashed toilets. A thick phlegm of filth, urine and cigarette ends bloated with moisture littered the floor.

'We all have fried chicken and salads here,' Sarge told

him, indicating the thick sludge of filth and urine in the toilet bowl. 'Here is what the mouth take in and the ass reject. You have a last chance to talk, or you will have to taste our fried chicken and salad.'

'Do as you like,' Challu said.

Sarge smiled and then exploded into action. He arched Challu's back downwards and plunged his head into the toilet bowl and kept it there for a while. When he pulled him back up Challu's head was like an incomplete mould of plaster.

'How fried chicken taste?'

'Like your mother.'

Then he did it again and again, each time with more bitterness and force. But still Challu would not talk.

He would not talk because he did not like Sarge's face and his display of power. He would not talk because it was a small act of resistance. He would not talk because he wanted to know that he had an inner strength to rely on.

Even when Sarge took him to an adjacent room and squeezed his testicles, then beat him on the balls of the feet with a staff, Challu's tongue remained obedient to his will. Sarge, though, was a hard man. He would not give up so easily.

When it grew dark, he took Challu outside the backyard of the police compound and stripped him of his clothes. A big ants' nest was under a mango tree. He raked it up, bound Challu's hands and legs with a cord and placed him on his buttocks amidst the raving insects. The ochre-coloured ants swarmed over his body and stung him madly with sharp needles of venom. Challu screamed in agony, but his will held out. He would not talk.

Sarge would still not give up. He made Challu open his legs and let the ants sting his private parts. But the pain of each torture made him more resolute and Sarge could not penetrate the barricade of Challu's will. He spat and fumed and kicked the soil in frustrated defeat. Challu's spirit glowed in triumph.

The defendant stood in the box, head hung loosely before him, immersed in his own thoughts. The magistrate read out the charge, 'Challu Gurwah are you guilty or are you not guilty?'

Challu's father looked at him with uncompromising scorn, his brother, Rudolph, shot him a look of seething hate. A sobbing trickled through the heavy breathing of the crowd gathered to hear the case. It was Challu's mother. Her eyes were fixed intently on her son, trying to signal to him that he should say 'Not guilty'.

'Is sin for a sin wrong?' Challu asked himself again. 'To commit a sin to earn a virtue wrong? Is violence for survival wrong?'

Then the splendour of his island came back to him: the beautiful river, the lovely fields, the festivals and the house he had burnt. The cycle of hatred had to be broken.

'Guilty, sir,' he said weakly.

A scream came from his mother.

The magistrate banged his mallet on the desk for order.

'Do you have anything to say?'

'No, sir.'

The prosecutor stood up and read out the charge again. The magistrate was writing assiduously in his ledger. Then he dropped the pen and looked at Challu austerely.

'Challu Gurwah, on account of the nature of your crime, you are sentenced to three years imprisonment.'

7

Under a pear tree, in an orange grove, two children were
playing with a lizard. The little girl wanted it, but the boy
wanted it more. The girl held the tail and the boy its head.
A bird flew across and the boy looked up. Seizing her
moment, the girl jerked it from him and scampered away.
The boy got up and tried to run after her. But he was slow
and awkward in his movements and, trying to move fas-
ter, he toppled over and fell down.

A woman from a nearby hut called out in alarm and ran
to pick him up. She shouted at the girl who giggled and
ran deeper into the grove. She came back with a man,
cowering behind him for protection against the woman's
wrath.

The man smiled. 'Don't whip her,' he told the woman.
'I'll catch another lizard.'

The man, the woman and the children sat under the
pear tree in the balmy shade of the branches, gazing down
the hill to the river covered with a brush of mangrove
trees.

'We been dreaming to come here, remember?' the
woman said.

'Now we is away from all the bad things of the past.'

She kissed him and her eyes were filled with tears.

'Remember the birds of the Waini River.'

The man put his hand on her shoulder. 'This place belongs to the birds. Maybe we've found somewhere far enough away from it all, the dog-eat-dog to survive, race against race, the Government against we all. Maybe here we find peace for a new beginning.'

Churaumanie Bissundyal was born in Guyana in 1950. He grew up on Leguan island on the Essequibo River. His father was a sea-defence labourer, his mother worked in the rice fields. He has worked as a school teacher deep in the interior of Guyana, as a civil servant and a National Insurance inspector. More recently, he has worked as a reviewer on the *Mirror* newspaper. He has researched Vedantic theosophy and taught Hindi.

Bissundyal has written three long narrative poems: *Glorianna*, *The Stream of Red Tears* and *The Cleavage*, published under the name of Omartelle Blessenequi. Since 1987 he has been heavily involved in theatre, writing and staging plays in Guyana, Jamaica and Canada. His plays include *The Trick and the Rajah, From Ganges to Demerary, The Migrant Error, The Jaguar and the Flute, I is a Jumbie, Hello Eldorado* and *Mad No Hell.*